More Than Love

Catherine Campbell

Dedicated to:

All the crazy beautiful women who have taught me something about love.

Once.
I was the fruit
clinging to the branch for dear life;
constantly in fear of autumn's coming -
that I might fall, shrivelled and dry,
untasted,
wasted.

Now.
I am the fruit
eager to ripen in all my delicious glory;
full of desire and anticipation
as I wait for your hands to choose me -
to save me from waste,
to savour my taste.

Introduction

At times I find the English language hopelessly inadequate to express the things I feel. Specifically, there are not enough adjectives to describe the diverse kinds of feelings love can provoke, or enough verbs to describe how one might like to act upon that love. The phrase 'I love you' itself feels overused and diluted to me, and isn't reserved exclusively for romantic love. I love flowers, I love Lady Gaga, I love birds, I love sun on my face, I love my dog, I love you. Saying I love those things doesn't really give anything away in terms of the depth or type of love I feel for each of them. The concept of love is vast, if not infinite, yet 'I love you' still seems to be the pinnacle of all statements used to verbally express romantic love. It can feel as though once you've told a person you love them, there's nothing else to say that could be more meaningful or significant. The poems in this collection are all inspired by romantic love, woman to woman. Each one is written from the premise of already knowing love is present, with a view to express something *beyond* that, to extend or deepen its meaning.

A Little About Me

As I was researching lesbians of history in order to share some of their musings in this book, I noticed one theme common to all. They all expressed feelings of not belonging in the world, as though they were somehow different to other humans. Anne Lister (1791-1840), who is often described as the 'first modern lesbian' quoted:

"I know my own heart and understand my fellow man. But I am made unlike anyone I have ever met. I dare to say I am like no one in the whole world."

Anne was a rarity in her day because she was openly lesbian and liberated. She even theatrically married her partner Ann Walker, at the Holy Trinity Church in York, now recognised as the birthplace of lesbian marriage in Britain. The way she remained authentic to her sexuality was courageous in her day, however it was never enough to make her feel at home in the world; she was still a rare thing who found no peace within the boundaries of social norms and expectations. Poets Virginia Woolf and Emily Dickenson are lesbians of history whose works also spoke of feeling isolated and trapped in a world that made little sense. Both become increasingly reclusive and suffered from mental illness throughout their lives. They were textbook tortured souls and much of it fed into their work.

I refer to these women because I feel they are my ancestral kindred spirits. I find it fascinating that the poets I've been most drawn to in my life were, or are, lesbians. I was immune to that fact at the time, as nothing about their poetry (at least what *I* was reading) spoke to sexuality, yet something in their words deeply resonated with me. In hindsight it feels as though I was attracted to them via ancestral radar signals; it's a mysterious thing. It makes sense *now* because I am one of them. For most of my life I too felt like a tortured soul losing myself in poetry and quietly drifting towards madness as my sense of not fitting into the world heightened. I thought either there was something wrong with the world or something wrong with me. I settled on the latter. In retrospect I'm almost certain my own mental illness (thankfully something I've since recovered from) stemmed from spending the vast majority of my life ignoring and suppressing who I really was and refusing to acknowledge even to myself what I truly desired. The soul torture I always felt came from not understanding the underlying reason I felt like a misfit.

As a child I was spoon fed the Catholic faith and had conservative British parents. My father was openly homophobic, so I grew up listening to his prejudices and judgements. I was shaped into a 'good' girl and diligently abided by the rules of my parents, the church and society at large. I left home at seventeen and the church was the first thing I shrugged off. For a long time I'd felt instinctively that some of the 'rules' made no sense because they suppressed freedom. I remember the day I stopped chanting by rote and instead *really* listened to what I'd been saying out loud in church all those years; I was shocked. Statements such as *I am not worthy*, and urging God's mother to *pray for my sins* so that when I died I wouldn't go to hell.

Though separating from the church was a positive start, I continued to swallow the expectations of my parents and society for many years, unaware they were slowly choking me. As a young adult it's not easy to recognise you've been brainwashed about life because all you know is what you've been told. Consequently, even after leaving home I continued to feel intermittently troubled about something feeling 'wrong.' It felt like there was *something* I didn't yet know or understand; *something* I hadn't been told.

I carried on with life, doing the expected, having relationships and sex with men. I was always a lot more sexual on my own than I ever was with a man, in an explorative, experimental kind of way. Perhaps that should have been an opening clue. I discovered how to pleasure myself from a young age so always felt sexually satisfied with or without a man. Still oblivious to my own needs and desires, I went on to do what any good, conservative girl 'should' do. I got married and had children.

Over those years, outside the normal course of developing deep and essential friendships with other females, there were times I encountered an intense connection with one. When it happened, it felt different to a 'normal' friendship in that I'd feel a heightened sense of anxiety around seeing them, despite an eagerness to do so. Where I'd ordinarily be confident in myself around both men and woman, I'd feel my pulse race and stumble on words in the presence of those particular women. Even then I never put two and two together. I labelled myself as being socially anxious around certain people, whatever the reason, which always baffled me. I didn't recognise it as falling in love.

It took me half a lifetime to evolve to a place where I could see through all the smoke screens and understand why everything had always felt displaced. It was liberating to finally learn I was not the person I'd been led to believe I was. The thing about being gay is it's *not* something anyone else can tell you; you have to figure it out alone. For me, it had been so difficult to land on because no-one around me and nothing in my world supported that truth. It's little wonder I didn't fit. I left my marriage, and everything changed.

After three years of personal growth and cathartic writing, I came out and ventured into the world of dating women. It was exciting in a petrifying kind of way. I knew wholeheartedly it's what I wanted as all the threads and clues woven throughout my life had tied together by then and the picture of me was clear. The clarity I had was such that it didn't matter if my coming out meant I'd lose anyone who'd walked beside me in life up to that point. I didn't care that my father was homophobic; that was his cross to bear - when I left my marriage I also divorced parental and societal expectations. The process of shedding all the worn, false layers of myself delivered me to personal liberation. All that remained was to have my first experience in the arms of a woman.

And so it was. And so it blew my mind every which way. All of a sudden, I fitted.

This book is a celebration of completing the journey back to my authentic self. I hope sharing these poems will help cultivate a sense of unity for others who are on the same journey. To *all* women, hope you will find inspiration within these pages to ignite fresh thoughts around expressing what you feel. I am deeply grateful that I've come to feel a sense of grounding and belonging. Since returned to myself, I have experienced so much **More than Love**.

Catherine Campbell

Table of Contents

Poetry

"How do I love thee? Let me count the ways.
I love thee to the depth and breadth and height
My soul can reach, when feeling out of sight.
For the ends of being and ideal grace.
I love thee to the level of every day's
Most quiet need, by sun and candlelight."

[Elizabeth Barrett Browning, 1850]

What Have You Done?

What have you done?

I have lost my senses,
as though everything I've ever known has departed me.
All I feel now is the deep tremor
of something restless and thunderous untethering inside;
a creature born with my first breath,
only to be swiftly banished into the dark depths of me…
starved of light and attention.

She was supposed to die.

What have you done?

I have lost my senses,
as though the world is still turning,
but I have stopped.
All I feel now is this creature unfurling,
stretching her majestic wings, rising, rising…
She has taken up all the space in me and we are breathing as one.
She is poised urgently, yet gracefully for liberty;
she can see the light; she can taste the attention.

She is very much alive.

What have you done?

Ripe for Picking

Once I was the fruit,
clinging to the branch for dear life;
constantly in fear of autumn's coming -
that I might fall, shrivelled and dry,
untasted,
wasted.

Now, I am the fruit
eager to ripen in all my delicious glory;
full of desire and anticipation
as I wait for your hands to choose me -
to save me from waste,
to savour my taste.

Intoxicated

I've swallowed a drug,
I think it's called *Love*.

It's making me crazy;
it's got me all fired,
it's making me hazy;
it's got me all wired.

I've swallowed a drug,
I think it's called *Love*.

It's got me a doozy;
it's making me wet,
it's got me all woozy;
it's making me sweat.

I've swallowed a drug,
I think it's called *Love*.

It's got me surrounded;
it's making me crush,
it's got me confounded;
it's making me flush.

I've swallowed a drug,
I think it's called *Love*.

It's making me fizzy;
it's under my skin,
it's making me dizzy,
it's got me *all in*.

I'm intoxicated,
whatever this is.

Heart Whispers

I watched you dance with willow trees,
fingers laced between their leaves.
Whispers murmured in my heart;
and *that's* the day I felt it start.

I watched you roam the fields for hours,
picking dainty wilder flowers.
My whispers grew in certainty;
this was love, in front of me.

I watched you kneel and touch the sand;
sift its treasures through your hand.
And darling, that's the day I *knew*,
I'd fallen
quite
in
love
with
you.

A Word from Anne

...take it from one who knew

"I could not sleep last night. Dozing, hot & disturbed ... a violent longing for a female companion came over me. I never remember feeling it so painfully before ... It was absolute pain to me."

[Anne Lister, 1823]

Jigsaws

Imagine we are both jigsaws, working on each other.
We started out by finding each other's corners and edges -
the outside pieces are always easiest to find.

Neither of us came with a reference picture,
because we don't yet know what we will become -
that will make some of the inside pieces challenging
to find and fit together.

As we continue, this is what I ask of you (as I will do for you):

Please don't give up if you can't find a middle piece of me.
It will be there somewhere, I promise -
because I am not one to hide pieces of myself;
not on purpose, anyway.
I need to know if a piece of me seems lost,
you'll help me find it,
so we can move closer to being complete.

If you can do that for me (as I will for you),
I will spill out all my inside pieces as they are,
and relax into getting excited about what we might become.

Elements

We are every element.

We are fire when our bodies come, together.
We are water in our depth and fluidity.
We are air lifting each other to heights unknown.
We are earth because through it all, we are grounded.

We are all these elements,
combined into a single element.

Let's call it W^2;
it's elementary.

[W^2 = Woman x Woman]

Feeling It All

I want to be inside you, so I can feel the cadence of your heart;
to know its ascension,
its peace.

I want to be inside you, so I can feel the tides of your joy;
to know its swell,
its retreat.

I want to be inside you, so I can feel the shades of your spirit;
to know its lightness,
its darkness.

I want to be inside you, so I can feel the surges of your fear;
to know its catalyst,
its calm.

I want to be inside you, so I can feel the rhythms of your desire;
to know its crescendo,
its climax.

I want to be inside you.
I want to feel it all.

A Word from Anne

...take it from one who knew

"I love and only love the fairer sex. My heart revolts from any other love than theirs. These feelings haven't wavered or deviated since childhood. I was born like this.

And I act as my God given nature dictates. If I was to lie with a man, surely that would be unnatural. Surely that would be against God. Who made us, every one of us. In all of our richness and variety."

[Anne Lister, 1831]

Insane Beauty

There is no denying you are insanely beautiful,
but you are not your body
to me –

you are the flowers you put in your hair when you're wandering
through the meadows

you are the paint on your cheek; the mark of your creativity
and playfulness at the end of a curious day

you are that old blue linen shirt you throw over yourself
on autumn mornings…
the one that hangs tantalisingly just so;
hovering on the edge of one of our sacred places

you are the tune you hum; unaware you are humming -
the sound you make, in the heights of your coming

you are all your books unread -
all your words unsaid

you are all these things and infinitely more.

Sometimes I'm so struck by the miracle of you,
I forget how insanely beautiful you are.

Were You Real?

Were you real, or trick of light,
a star that shot across the night?

Did you exist in conscious time,
were those your hands entwined with mine?

Were you a puff of smoke long gone,
were those your lips I lingered on?

Were you a spell, was I entranced,
were those your arms in which I danced?

It all feels like a dream somehow,
our longing in the slipstream now.

All that's left is how I feel…
proof enough, that you were real.

New Beginnings

Before we continue…
I don't want to read between the lines with you,
or find I'm reading a different book altogether.
I've never enjoyed trying to guess another person's story.
It's exhausting.

I want us to sit together and open a floral journal…
inhale the intoxicating scent of new pages,
and write our love story in collaboration.
Our writing companions will be truth, vulnerability, and humour.

Parts of our story will be wild and hilarious;
parts will be thrilling and unexpected;
parts will be intimate and sensual;
and parts will be intellectual and deadly serious -
because we are all those things, you and me.
It won't be a drama.
It will be a rom-com erotic thriller.

We won't know the end until it comes,
but we have our beginning…
we have our BEGINNING!

A Word from Emily

...take it from one who knew

"Susie, will you indeed come home next Saturday, and be my own again, and kiss me as you used to? (...) I hope for you so much and feel so eager for you, feel that I cannot wait, feel that now I must have you—that the expectation once more to see your face again, makes me feel hot and feverish, and my heart beats so fast (...) my darling, so near I seem to you, that I disdain this pen, and wait for a warmer language."

[Emily Dickenson, 1852]

I'm Yours

I don't need you to buy me expensive flowers...
but pick me a wildflower as we walk hand-in-hand
through the woods,
and I'm *Yours*

I don't need you to adorn me with a diamond ring...
but find a beautiful shell on the beach
and slip it on my finger with a kiss,
and I'm *Yours*

I don't need you to whisk me away to a luxury retreat...
but pack us a picnic and a soft old rug
to lay down where the birds sing,
and I'm *Yours*

I don't need you to take me elaborate shows…
but take me in your arms and dance with me
when no-one is looking,
and I'm *Yours*

Speak to me in the language of my love…
in gestures not grandeur,
and I'm *Yours*

The Magic of You

You're like that magical wand photo edit feature on an iPhone;
the one that makes everything brighter and richer in colour.

The presence of you turns rather ordinary things
into something quite extraordinary.

The lines of the world are cleaner and sharper,
the full moon is fuller, somehow.
I'm noticing the graceful intricacy and beauty of flowers;
the patient and effortless magnificence of nature.
The grass is greener,
the sea is bluer,
the air is lighter,
the stars are brighter.

That's the magic of You.

The Moment

I remember the exact moment I fell into you.

You were taking us off on an adventure.
I looked over at you while you were driving
and saw that ever so soft smile of yours -
twinkling eyes focused forward,
driving carefully and mindfully as always.

I could see in that moment,
you were experiencing serene happiness.
In that same moment, I felt a rush of love for you
and was deeply grateful to be a passenger of your joy.

Whenever we go adventuring
I always sneak a sideways look at that smile of yours,
and it still makes me feel the same way.

A Word to Virginia

...take it from one who knew

"I am reduced to a thing that wants Virginia. I composed a beautiful letter to you in the sleepless nightmare hours of the night, and it has all gone. I just miss you, in a quite simple desperate human way. I miss you even more than I could have believed; and I was prepared to miss you a good deal. So this letter is just really a squeal of pain. It is incredible how essential to me you have become. I suppose you are accustomed to people saying these things. Damn you, spoilt creature; I shan't make you love me any the more by giving myself away like this—But oh my dear, I can't be clever and stand-offish with you: I love you too much for that. Too truly. You have no idea how stand-offish I can be with people I don't love. I have brought it to a fine art. But you have broken down my defences."

V.

[Vita Sackville-West in a letter to Virginia Woolf]

What You Are

You're diamond gold, a doublet jewel;
High Priestess and doubtless fool.
Iron fist in velvet glove -
nothing that is not to love.

You're wolf inside a cuddly sheep;
anchor in the daunting deep.
Lion mixed with tender dove -
nothing that is not to love.

You're dandelion and ancient tree;
yin and yang in symphony.
Rising sun and shooting star -
nothing not to love, you are.

If You See Her

If you see my girl, please tell her I love her.

She'll be barefoot in a meadow somewhere, picking wildflowers.
There will be one tucked behind her left ear.
Her hair is the colour of a black robin's chest
and her eyes blaze peacock blue.

Birds will be singing nearby.

She'll be wearing something white.
It will be light and elegant; something she can be free in.
She'll move about gracefully with a far-away look on her face,
as if she knows secret things and is more than just her body.

You'll know it, when you see her,
because a kind of warmth will fall over you
and you'll question everything you thought you knew.

Anyway, if you see my girl, please tell her I love her.

Why?

Why, Oh, Why -
do I keep falling for falling in love,
keep believing it will be weightless and heavenly
even when it has nearly crushed me?

Because it's always worth it.
It's *always* worth it.

A Word from Emily

...take it from one who knew

"I think of love, and you, and my heart grows full and warm, and my breath stands still...

I can feel a sunshine stealing into my soul and making it all summer, and every thorn a rose."

[Emily Dickenson]

More Of You

I want to map much more of you,
explore you *everywhere* -
find the most exquisite parts, and dare to take you there.

I want to hold much more of you,
press your flesh to mine -
sink into your skin until our naked hearts align.

I want to feel much more of you,
traverse you head to toe -
fingers searching gently for the parts you'd have me know.

I want to taste much more of you,
my mouth across your skin -
cover all your surfaces, then slowly move within.

I want to see much more of you,
examine every piece -
take you to desire's edge, then watch as you release.

No Words

I can't tell you how much I love you,
I can't find the words, literally.

I've tried stringing words together in elaborate ways,
but our language is hopelessly inadequate.

The thing about love, it's a *feeling*.
If you could *feel* me, you'd know.
I hope you feel me darling.

Anyway, you'll just have to trust me when I say,
I can't tell you how much I love you.

Snow White

At first I thought she was like Snow White
who occasionally disguised herself as a wolf.
Other times I thought she was like a wolf
who occasionally disguised herself as Snow White.

Now I've come to love her,
I see she is both.
She can be deadly fierce
and as soft as falling snow.

I love them both.

A Word from Anne

...take it from one who knew

"I do not like to be too long estranged from you sometimes, for, Mary, there is a nameless tie in that soft intercourse which blends us into one & makes me feel that you are mine. There is no feeling like it. There is no pledge which gives such sweet possession."

[Anne Lister, 1823]

Little Things

Silky sheets and satin slips, gifts with Midas touch -
lavish weekend whisk-always; it's all a bit too much.

It's not that I'm ungrateful, I love the things you do,
but *little things* are all I need to fall in love with you.

Serenades and diamonds, robes of velvet touch -
flowers and fancy perfumes; it's all a bit too much.

It's not that I'm ungrateful, I love the things you do,
but *little things* are all I need to fall in love with you.

Little things, like hold my hand and walk with me a while,
Little things, like catch my eye and share a knowing smile.

Little things, like knowing when I need a cup of tea,
Little things, like cuddling while we're watching the T.V.

Little things, like kiss my head or send a cheeky wink,
Little things, like share your thoughts and ask me what I think.

It's *little things* that matter, for love is not to strive.
Little things are all I need to keep our love alive.

Anything For You

When I say I'd do anything for you, I mean it.

There's no grief more crushing than a broken heart,
no loss more desolate than love sundered.
Yet I've allowed myself to fall in love with you *anyway*.

So there you have it;
I'm willing to do *anything* for you.

Dichotomy

Your body is a dichotomy.

So demure and tasteful disguised in corporate clothing,
but oh so suggestive and sensuous underneath.

So delicate and smooth under my soft caress,
but oh so formidable and electric in the heights of ecstasy.

Your body has me captivated,
but Oh!
Your body has me liberated.

A Word from Anne

...take it from one who knew

"I am not made like any other I have seen.
I dare believe oneself to be different from any other who exist."

[Anne Lister, 1823]

Always You

I've carried you in my heart
since the notion of love first dawned upon me.
You comforted me when I became lost in melancholy,
deeply saddened by a world I didn't fit into.
I loved you before I knew you.

I've carried you in my heart
even as others have entered and left.
You calmed me when I became unmoored,
desperate to escape from the shallowness of reality.
I loved you before I knew you.

I've carried you in my heart
through all the times I have been alone.
You reassured me when I became isolated,
unwilling to participate in the great show of life.
I loved you before I knew you.

And now my love, you are here.
Welcome to my heart -
we've been waiting for you.

Rising In Love

What an odd expression it is,
to say one *falls* in love -
to imply one is lowered or less, somehow.

Is it not more fitting, more hopeful,
to say one *rises* in love -
to imply one is lifted,
that one might ascend to heights unknown?

I think so.
In which case I am rising in love with you sweet girl.

Creating Us

You are YOU,
I am ME,
Together, we're an Entity.

WE is altogether new -
I'm still ME,
and you're still YOU.

We are conscious creators, mindful curators.
We are responsible for our own becoming.

And when WE become,
YOU and ME must nurture our creation,
for the entity will be young and vulnerable.
She will think she's all grown up,
but will need us to watch over and care for her.
YOU and ME are the only ones
who can guide her towards her fullness…
and we must do this without becoming less full ourselves.

A Word from Anne

...take it from one who knew

"Oh, women, women!
I am always taken up with some girl or other."

[Anne Lister, 1824]

Orgasmic Osmosis

What I feel as I allow myself to melt into you
is a longing beyond comparison.

The way you hold me as I am coming,
is an intimacy beyond comparison.

What I feel when that longing is liberated,
is the deepest pleasure I will ever know.

The way we become *one* in that moment -
it's orgasmic osmosis.

Some Things I Love

I love it when you can't find a pair of clean socks,
but know exactly where to find mine and help yourself.

I love seeing your shoes at the front door,
all higgledy-piggledy, very much at home.

I love that you know where to find all the bits and bobs,
like paperclips and batteries
and the special stick to unblock the coffee machine.

I love seeing your toothbrush in the bathroom,
your shirt peeking out from under the pillow,
the enormous pile books on your side of the bed.

More than anything,
I love feeling you next to me in bed at night.
I *really* love that.

I still can't quite believe you're here.

Desire

Oh my God.

When I close my eyes to reimagine the sounds of your coming,
something very physical happens at the core of my sacral chakra.

It isn't pain,
It isn't delight.
It isn't an ache,
It isn't butterflies.

It's like a slow, deep turning,
then an instant where it catches…
like the final click of a vault being cracked -

Then it happens.

I am flooded -
overwhelmed with pure and sacral desire.
It is a feeling like no other.

Oh. My. God.

A Word from Virginia

...take it from one who knew

"Love, the poet said, is woman's whole existence."

[Virginia Woolf]

The Lotus

You unfold me,
one petal at a time
until I *become*…
just as the lotus flower blooms
in all her
vulnerable
magnificent
wholeness.

Done Me Over

You really did a number on me;
worked me over good and proper.
You led me down the garden path
and wrapped me around your little finger
until I was completely taken in.

I loved it.
Do it again.

What I Really Mean

When we're apart and I send you this message in the morning,
"Have a good day darling,"
what I *really* mean is:

I hope you love yourself today.
I hope you find joy in the smallest of things.
I hope you find a reason for your eyes to twinkle.
I hope the people around you make you feel happy.
I hope you smile and laugh.
I hope you stay well and safe.
Remember I love you.

When we're apart and I send you this message in the evening,
"Sleep well darling,"
what I *really* mean is:

I hope you went to bed happy.
I hope you are feeling cosy.
I hope you fall asleep quickly.
I hope nothing is worrying you, that might keep you up.
I hope if you have dreams, they are beautiful.
I hope you feel rested in the morning.
Remember I love you.

Come Now

Come, come now darling,
empty your mind and open your body;
permit your lips to crush on me;
offer your tongue the taste of me;
allow your flesh to quiver with me -
Come, come now darling.

Inside Out

Clothed in body,
naked and vulnerable in spirit,
when we began.

And you,
my beautiful girl,
did exactly what I needed you to do.
You nourished me from the inside out;
loved my soul before you loved my body.

So it wasn't limerence,
it wasn't lust;
it was Love!

No… it was

More

Than

Love.

Ones Who Knew

Love is as old as humanity.
It has been the muse of poets, artists, thinkers,
musicians, and all creators through all of time.

We all know.
We've always known.
We always will.

Anne Lister

Anne Lister was born in 1791. She was androgynous in appearance and dressed only in black. Though she was a landowner and successful businesswoman, her place in history stems from her penning of a five-million-word diary. Her musings included thoughts about social, political, and economic events of the time, but she also wrote a great deal about her sexuality, including explicit and graphic details about her life as a lesbian.

She started writing her diary when she was fifteen, which coincided with her first lesbian affair with school friend Eliza Raine. They created a secret code using mathematical symbols, the Greek alphabet, zodiac, and punctuation, which they used to write and decipher love letters they sent each other.

As evident in her writing, Anne was always open about her sexuality and lived authentically. She had two significant relationships in her lifetime, the first being with Mariana Lawton which lasted for almost twenty years. Mariana was married for much of that time but her husband was aware of, and resigned to, her affair with Anne.

Anne's final relationship was with Ann Walker which lasted until Anne died from a fever in 1840. In 1834, the lovers had a non-legal marriage ceremony on Easter Sunday at the Holy Trinity Church in York. Today the church is recognised as being the site of the first lesbian marriage held in Britain. In 2018, a blue and rainbow plaque was unveiled at the church to honour Lister and her union with Ann. It was York's first LGBT plaque. It reads:

Anne Lister
1791 – 1840
of Shibden Hall, Halifax
Lesbian and Diarist;
took sacrament here to seal her
union with Ann Walker
Easter 1834

[Information and image from Wikipedia: Anne Lister]

Emily Dickenson

Born in 1830, Emily Dickenson was an American poet. Her fame was posthumous as her poetry only became public after her death in 1886, when her sister discovered her cache of poems and published them.

It can't be stated as fact, but many scholars who have studied Emily's work believe her lifelong relationship with sister-in-law Susan Gilbert was a romantic one. When her poems were discovered, several were written about Susan, expressing strong homoerotic feelings. Prior to publication of those specific poems, the publisher censored Susan's name and replaced it with a man's name to conceal evidence of a lesbian romance. Emily's relationship with Susan is explored in the 2018 movie "Wild Nights with Emily" and also inspired the television series "Dickenson" (2019 – 2021).

[Information and image from Wikipedia: Emily Dickenson]

Virginia Woolf

Virginia was born in 1882 and suffered from mental health issues throughout her life. In 1941 she drowned herself by walking into a fast-flowing river with a heavy stone in her pocket.

She was a founding member of the Bloomsbury Group, formed in 1905 and hosted at the home she shared with her artist sister, Vanessa. The group brought together artists, writers, and intellectuals to support each other's creative activities and held very progressive views regarding sexuality. The majority of its members were openly queer.

While Virginia married, she was frank with her husband about not wanting to have sex with him, which was thought to be influenced by sexual abuse she suffered as a child at the hands of men. This is a quote from a letter she wrote to her husband Leonard in 1912 just prior to their marriage:

"I sometimes think that if I married you, I could have everything - and then - is it the sexual side of it that comes between us? As I told you brutally the other day, I feel no physical attraction in you."

The significant love affair of her life was with Vita Sackville-West who she met in 1922. Vita was also married and a popular writer of the time. As well as inspiring each other in a professional capacity, Virginia and Vita's relationship was passionate and sexual. This is depicted in the hundreds of poetic letters they wrote to each other throughout the course of their relationship. Virginia's love for Vita inspired one of her most famous novels, "Orlando," published in 1928.

The movie "Vita & Virginia" was released in 2019, which is based on their relationship and uses actual content from their love letters in its script.

[Information and image from Wikipedia: Virginia Woolf]

Something More

Carry gracefully into your future love
the wisdom you gained
from the pain of lost loves…
and your love will evermore
be heightened with each new experience.

Something More Series

More Than Love is part of a two-book series. It's partner is **More Than Pain**.

All of life is a dichotomy. Peace and War. Joy and Sorrow. Light and Dark, Love and Pain. Life and Death. As humans beings, we cannot escape this reality. To be alive is to experience it all.

There are always two sides to a story when it comes to relationships, and they might be very different. Most likely they both begin with love and end in pain, but will be a myriad of both and every other kind of emotion in between. We all feel and respond to emotions uniquely. Some are cautious in love while others catapult into it headfirst. Some express pain openly and outwardly, while others turn inward and seek privacy. What's common to us all is that we're caught up in the cyclical nature of the human experience. Love and pain are partners in life. The cost of love is deferred pain. The gift of pain, if we embrace it, is wisdom. And wisdom is a pathway to love.

More Than Love and **More Than Pain** can be read in any order. In union they represent hope and all that is good. When we allow ourselves to really feel an emotion, whether positive or negative, we gift ourselves an opportunity to grow and learn.

More Than Pain is available on Amazon, alongside it's partner.

Thankyou

The process of writing this book has brought me a lot of pleasure, as I hope the reading of it has brought you.

I would love to travel in time and have a cup of tea with Emily or Virginia. Or Mary Oliver, another of my favourite (also lesbian) poets who passed away recently. I'm thankful I was able to share some of their musings, as well as Anne Listers, due to their work now being in the public domain. I'm also grateful that in the process of writing **More Than Love** I learned more about these incredible women and the part they played in both the history of writing and LGBTQ rights.

Some of the poems in this book are inspired by my own romantic relationships with women, others through simply 'knowing' and permitting myself to conjure feelings through sensuous imaginings. One thing I've learned since coming out is that while we all share a love of women, we are all unique, so no one union or experience is like any other. My goal in writing and sharing this book is to reach and touch other kindred spirits to unite us in Love, and **More**.

I'm very grateful you are here.

If you enjoyed **More Than Love** I invite you to leave a review on Amazon and share the poem/s that resonated with you the most.

Catherine Campbell

Printed in Great Britain
by Amazon